Nadim and Anneena came to play at Biff and Chip's house. Nadim had a book about the Ancient Egyptians.

"It isn't just a book to read," said Nadim. "It's a special sort of book."

1

"It's a model book," said Nadim.

He opened it to show everyone.

"I get it," said Chip. "You press out the shapes.
Then you fold and glue them to make a model."

The book had lots of shapes to press out and
fold. Nadim pointed to one.

"Can you see what this will be?" he asked.

"Of course we can," said Anneena. "It will be
a pyramid."

Chip found some glue. Then Nadim pressed out the shapes and the others began to fold them. First they made the pyramids. Anneena had a difficult shape to fold.

"This is a sphinx," she said.

They pressed out some tiny trees and people.
Biff glued them all on to a sheet of paper. It made
a scene of Ancient Egypt. The children were
pleased with it.

"I'm really pleased with the sphinx," said
Anneena.

At last the model was finished. It looked so good they called Mum upstairs to have a look.

"What a good job you made of it," said Mum. "I like the pyramids and the sphinx."

"The sphinx was hard to make," said Anneena.

Floppy ran into the room. He didn't see the model on the floor and he trod on it with his big paws. He knocked over a tree and crushed the sphinx.

"Oh Floppy!" everyone yelled.

Floppy looked unhappy. He knew he had
upset the children.

"Never mind," said Chip. "It wasn't Floppy's
fault. The sphinx looks even better than before."

Suddenly the magic key began to glow. The key took the children back in time. It took Floppy too.

"It's not my day!" thought Floppy. "First, I get into trouble. Now, it's a magic adventure."

The magic took them back to Ancient Egypt.
They were standing by a pyramid. The pyramid
was still being built. Far off they could see two
more pyramids.

"This is amazing!" said Nadim. "I didn't think
the pyramids were so big."

Some people were pulling on long ropes.
They were moving a big block of stone.

"That's amazing too," said Chip. "I didn't
know the pyramids were made with such big
blocks of stone."

"Look over there!" gasped Anneena. She pointed to a huge stone sphinx. "Let's go and look at the sphinx," she said.
They all began to run towards it. Floppy didn't go with them. He had seen a cat!

The cat hissed at Floppy. Floppy couldn't stop himself. He chased it! It leaped on to some blocks of stone. Floppy jumped up too, but the cat was too fast for him.

Biff saw Floppy chase the cat. She called to the others. They all went back to get Floppy, but he was stuck on the blocks of stone. He couldn't get down.

"Oh Floppy! You silly dog," said Biff.

The children looked up at Floppy.

"He's a long way up!" laughed Nadim.

"I'll just have to climb up and help him down," said Biff.

Then a man ran over. He looked at Floppy and gasped.

The man called to some people. They ran over
to the children. At first they were talking and
shouting. Then they all went quiet.

"What are they doing?" asked Biff. "Why are
they looking at us like this?"

The people put their hands together and raised them in the air. Then they sank down on their knees.

"They are bowing to us," said Chip. "They must think we're important."

"How strange!" said Nadim.

The people were not bowing down to the children. They were bowing to Floppy.

"I don't believe it!" whispered Chip. "They must think Floppy is important. I wonder why?"

The people took Floppy away. The children
followed. Floppy couldn't believe all this was
happening to him.

"A magic adventure is bad enough," he thought,
"and now this!"

The people took Floppy to the king's palace.
The king came out on to the steps.

"In Egypt a king is called a pharaoh,"
said Chip. "This pharaoh looks very fierce."
Everyone bowed when they saw him.

"We'd better bow down, too" said Biff.
"We don't want to get into trouble."
A man spoke to the pharaoh.

"Great Pharaoh!" he said. "See what we have
brought."

"The yellow dog!" gasped the pharaoh.

The pharaoh took Floppy inside the palace. Then he clapped his hands.

"Look after the yellow dog," he said. "Give him whatever he wants."

"Hmm!" thought Floppy. "I'm beginning to enjoy this adventure."

"I just don't get it," said Biff. "Why are they making this fuss of Floppy?"
The pharaoh clapped his hands again. Some people ran into the palace. One of them began to paint a picture of Floppy.

Suddenly Biff sneezed. The pharaoh saw the children.

"Strangers in my palace," he shouted. "How did they get in?"

A guard grabbed Chip and Anneena. Another one grabbed Biff and Nadim.

The guards took the children outside. They took them to one of the pyramids. The people were moving the big blocks of stone.

"You all look strong," said a guard. "You can work here."

The children had to help pull one of the big blocks. They had to put rollers down to slide it along.

"This is hard work," moaned Biff. "These rollers are heavy."

It was time for a rest. The children had to drink from a skin bag.

"Ugh!" said Chip. "This water is warm and it tastes funny too. I'd rather have an ice-cold can."

The Egyptians were carving a giant stone block. The children had to pick up all the chips of stone that fell off.

"This is hard work, too," said Nadim.

"It's no fun being an Egyptian slave."

Anneena looked at the carving.

"I wonder if they are making a sphinx?"
she said. "A sphinx has the body of a lion but
that doesn't look like a lion's tail."

"Hmm! That tail looks familiar," said Biff.

The carving was finished.

"I said it looked familiar," gasped Biff. "It isn't a sphinx at all – it's Floppy."

At that moment the pharaoh came to see the carving. Some Egyptians carried Floppy.

Suddenly the magic key began to glow. Floppy jumped down and ran over to the children.

"Come back, yellow dog," called the pharaoh.

"I'm glad it's time to go," thought Floppy. "It was all getting too much of a good thing."

"What an adventure," said Nadim. "I didn't like being an Egyptian slave."

Anneena picked up the model sphinx.

"A sphinx has a lion's body and a man's head," she said. "But this does look a bit like Floppy."